Archie at the Museum

First published in 2012
by Wayland

Wayland
338 Euston Road
London NW1 3BH

Wayland Australia
Level 17/207 Kent Street
Sydney, NSW 2000

Series Editor: Louise John
Series design: Paul Cherrill
Design: Lisa Peacock
Consultant: Shirley Bickler

A CIP catalogue record for this book is available from the British Library.

ISBN 9780750268684

Printed in China

Wayland is a division of Hachette Children's Books,
an Hachette UK Company

www.hachette.co.uk

Archie at the Museum

Written by Anne Rooney
Illustrated by Ann Johns

WAYLAND

"Hurry up and get on the bus, everyone," Miss Nitwit called. Archie pushed Camilla out of the way and got on first.

"Right, Archie. You can sit next to me!" said Miss Nitwit.

Archie hated sitting next to
Miss Nitwit. He had to sit still.
And he could not pick his nose.
He took out his sandwich and
he squeezed out some jam.

"Look, Miss, I'm a vampire!"
said Archie.

"Don't be silly. Put your lunch
away!" Miss Nitwit said.

At the museum, they went into the dinosaur hall. They saw moving dinosaurs that roared.

"Are they real?" Camilla asked Miss Nitwit.

"Those skeletons are real,"
said Miss Nitwit, "but these
dinosaurs are just models."

"That's not true," Archie roared.
"They are all real. Watch out
or they'll eat you!"

Camilla started to cry.
Everyone ran around
pretending to be dinosaurs.

"Be quiet!" said Miss Nitwit.
"Or we'll have to leave."

Archie ran into a dinosaur
skeleton. A big bone fell off.

"Come along, everyone,"
called Miss Nitwit. "Time to
look at the fossils."

Archie didn't want to look
at fossils. He hid behind a
big dinosaur.

Then he climbed up to the
dinosaur display.

Archie lay down in front of a roaring dinosaur. It waved its legs and moved its head up and down. It had sharp teeth.

Archie got his sandwiches.
He squeezed out the jam and
wiped it on his face.

Then he waited.

Miss Nitwit counted up
the children.

"Where is Archie?" she
asked. "Camilla, please go
and look for him in the
dinosaur hall."

Camilla did as she was told.
She always did as she was told.

The dinosaurs were so scary. There was a big bone on the floor. Maybe they were real, just like Archie said!

Camilla heard the dinosaurs roaring. She didn't want to go near them at all.

The dinosaurs were still moving, still roaring and still eating...

Wait! One of them was eating Archie! He was covered in red stuff.

"Help! Help!" Archie screamed. "The dinosaur is eating me up!"

Camilla ran to Miss Nitwit.

"Miss! Miss! Come quickly!
A dinosaur is eating Archie!"
she shouted.

She held onto Miss Nitwit's leg, crying.

Everyone ran to see Archie being eaten. Miss Nitwit just walked slowly.

In the dinosaur hall, Archie was screaming.

"Archie's head is bleeding!" sobbed Camilla. "We are all going to be eaten!"

Miss Nitwit was very cross
with Archie. "Archie, get out
of there now!" she shouted.

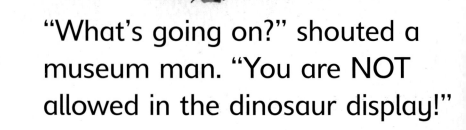

"What's going on?" shouted a museum man. "You are NOT allowed in the dinosaur display!"

The man switched the dinosaurs off. Archie was still screaming, but the dinosaurs had stopped moving.

"Oh!" Archie said.

Archie had to clean the jam
off the dinosaur. All of it.

He had to sit and wait on the
museum steps all by himself.

Miss Nitwit was very cross.
"That's it, Archie!" she said.
"You are NOT coming on the
next school trip!"

"Oh, Archie, you are awful!"
said Camilla.

START READING is a series of highly enjoyable books for beginner readers. The books have been carefully graded to match the Book Bands widely used in schools. This enables readers to be sure they choose books that match their own reading ability.

Look out for the Band colour on the book in our Start Reading logo.

The Bands are:

Pink Band 1

Red Band 2

Yellow Band 3

Blue Band 4

Green Band 5

Orange Band 6

Turquoise Band 7

Purple Band 8

Gold Band 9

START READING books can be read independently or shared with an adult. They promote the enjoyment of reading through satisfying stories supported by fun illustrations.

Anne Rooney has written lots of books for children including the All About Henry stories for this series. Have a look! She lives in a state of chaos with her two daughters, a tortoise called Tor2 and a blue lobster called Marcel.

Ann Johns likes to draw life – busy, lovely life. Birds flying, dogs jumping, people dancing... So always have a pencil handy, because you never know what exciting thing is waiting around the corner for you to draw!